These doughnuts belong to:

....

Doughnuts

To Nan and Frank

First published in the UK in 2015 by Hodder Children's Books
This edition published in 2015

Text and illustrations copyright © Steve Antony 2015

Hodder Children's Books
An imprint of Hachette Children's Group
Part of Hodder & Stoughton
Carmelite House
50 Victoria Embankment
London EC4Y 0DZ

A catalogue record of this book is available from the British Library.

ISBN: 978 1 444 91665 2
Printed in China

An Hachette UK Company

www.hachette.co.uk

Hodder
Children's
Books

A division of Hachette Children's Group

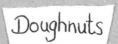

Doughnuts

Please Mr Panda

Steve Antony

Would you like a doughnut?

Give me the pink one.

No, you can not have a doughnut.
I have changed my mind.

Would you like a doughnut?

I want
the blue one
and
the yellow one.

No, you can not have a doughnut.
I have changed my mind.

Would you like a doughnut?

Would you like a doughnut?

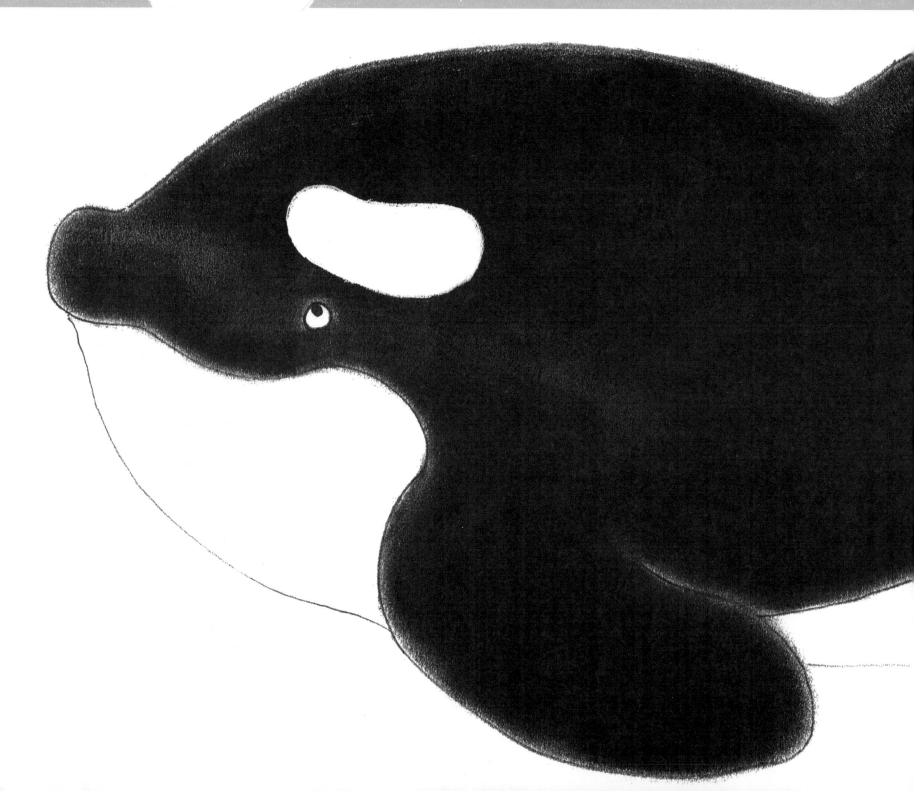

I want them all!

Then bring me some more.

No, you can not have a doughnut.
I have changed my mind.

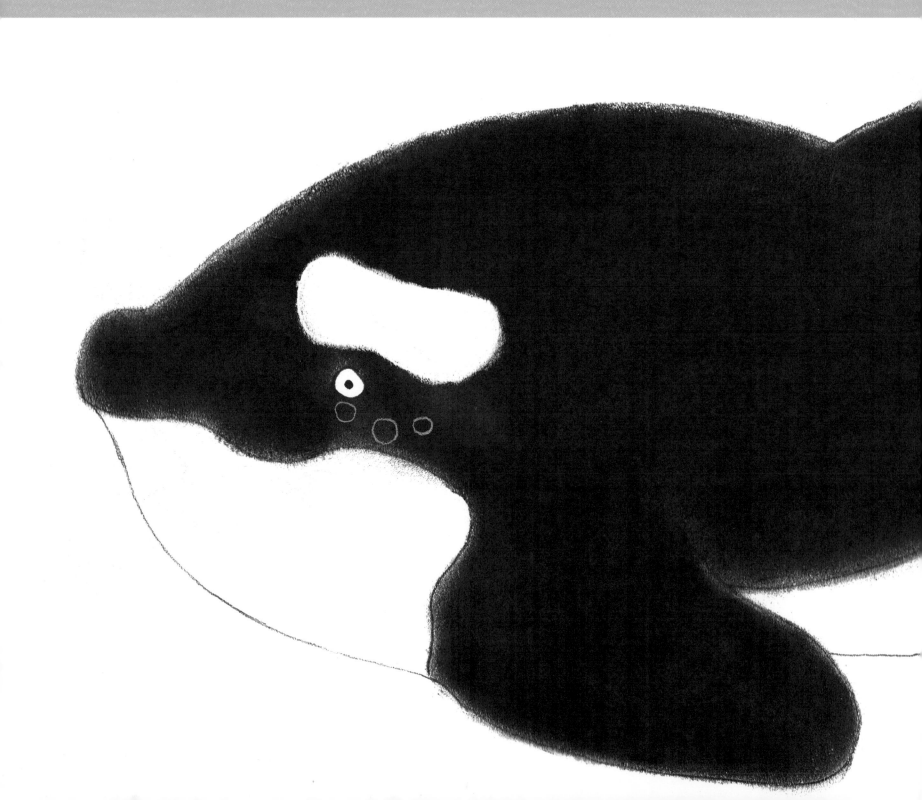

Would anyone else like a doughnut?

Hello!
May I have a doughnut...

Please

Mr Panda.

You can have them all.

Thank you very much!

I love doughnuts.

You're welcome.
I don't like doughnuts.

Also by *Steve Antony*: